4/2015

To Jonathan

From The Weinbergers

The Long Ride

A CHILD'S SEARCH

DON REGIER

ILLUSTRATED BY KAREN PRITCHETT

Text © 2004 by Don Regier
Illustrations © 2004 by Karen Pritchett

Published by Kregel Kidzone, an imprint of Kregel Publications, P.O. Box 2607, Grand Rapids, MI 49501.

Art Direction / Interior Design: John M. Lucas
ISBN 0-8254-3577-3
Printed in China

04 05 06 07 08 / 5 4 3 2 1

Where Kids are number One

Once upon a time on the other side of the world, there lived two beautiful little girls with black hair, button noses, and bright eyes as black as coal.

Bei Bei and Li Li weren't sisters, but they were good friends. They lived in a big house with lots of other boys and girls, mostly girls. They slept together in the same bed. They ran and played with their friends.

But something was missing.

They didn't have a mommy to sing to them or wipe away their tears. There was no daddy to bounce them on his knee. They had no big brother or sister to take them to the ice-cream store.

Then something happened that was a little scary and very wonderful.

Early one morning, the nurse awakened the sleeping girls. "Come on, sleepy-heads," she said. "We're going for a long ride."

As they got ready, the nurse told them something very exciting. "Today you will meet your new family."

"What's a family?" wondered Li Li. "What does a family look like? Can I bounce on it? Does it make pretty music or funny sounds? Does it taste yummy? Is a family soft? Is it something I can hold and cuddle? Will it keep me warm?"

A man on a big tricycle stopped in front of the big house. The nurse helped the girls climb onto the seat. Li Li tried to bounce up and down on it, but it was hard like a board. "Is this a family?" she asked.

"No, no," laughed the nurse. "This is a pedicab. You just wait, and soon you will see your family."

When the long ride in the pedicab ended, the girls tumbled out.

They rubbed their eyes and stared at something that was long and noisy and full of people. "Oh, this must be a family," thought Li Li. But it didn't make pretty music. It only made a screeching noise.

"Is this my family?" she asked.

The nurse smiled and said, "No, this isn't a family. It's just a train."

The long train bumped and jolted through the countryside. Li Li wondered when the long ride would end. "It's taking too long," she whimpered. Bei Bei started to cry, so the nurse hugged her and carried her back and forth in the crowded train.

The slow-moving train stopped at every little town. Villagers crowded around the open windows and sold food to the tired travelers. The nurse bought a special treat for the girls. Li Li was sure that this must be a family, because it tasted so yummy, but the nurse called it a banana.

At the end of the long ride the train hissed to a stop in a big city. The nurse said it was the capital city, but the girls didn't know what a capital was.

They had never seen so many people before, or so many airplanes in the sky. The nurse said that maybe their family was in one of those airplanes.

"But how can a family be in such a tiny thing up in the sky?" Li Li thought. "A family must be something very small."

Next they took a long ride in a car. The nurse called it a "taxi." The noisy taxi tooted its horn so it wouldn't bump into the buses or the people who were riding their bicycles in the street.

"Could a family be on a bike?" Li Li wondered. "Could it be in a bus?"

Finally the taxi stopped at the biggest house the girls had ever seen. Was this a family? No, the nurse called it a "hotel."

Could a family be inside a hotel?

People were standing inside the big hotel looking at the girls. Some of the people had cameras with bright flashing lights in front of their faces.

A man in a fancy suit opened the big glass door, and out came a mommy with golden hair, a daddy with hair that looked like salt and pepper, and a big sister who said, "My dream has come true! At last I have two little sisters."

"So this is a family," thought Li Li. "But I hoped that I could bounce on it, or that it would make pretty music, or that it would taste yummy. I thought maybe it would be soft, and I could cuddle it."

And then the daddy took Li Li on his lap. He bounced her on his knee and said, "Hupps, hupps, hupps."

The mommy took Bei Bei on her lap and sang softly. Bei Bei couldn't understand the strange words. Not yet. But she thought the music was very pretty.

The sister gave the girls a yummy drink of warm milk and a soft little toy lamb. She cuddled them close for a long time.

Then the girls knew that they had found what they had wanted all along—a family. And they learned that a family loves you just as you are—even if you're poor, or hungry or thirsty, or even if you're sick.

And a family will never stop loving you. Never.

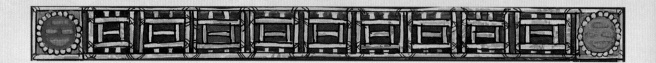

Later that night, after Li Li and Bei Bei had a nice warm bath, Daddy said, "Our little babies remind me of something in God's book, the Bible. It says 'All of us have strayed away like sheep. We have left God's paths to follow our own' (Isaiah 53:6). That means that people are lost and far away from God's family."

"Like little lost lambs," said Mommy.

"Or like orphans," said Daddy. "Just as the big ocean separated Li Li and Bei Bei from our family, the Bible says that our sin separates each of us from God and His family. Life is sad when we are far away from God."

"I remember what it was like to be away from God," said Mommy, and her eyes filled with tears.

Then the daddy smiled a big smile. "But God came looking for us. Because of what He did, everyone can leave their sad lives and be adopted into His family."

"Just like we adopted Li Li and Bei Bei," Sister said. "Mommy, do you think they know that God wants to adopt them, too?"

The mommy smiled. "They will know," she said. "We will tell them about all the work God did for them and about how much He loves them."

"I want them to know how much we wanted them in our family and that we worked very hard to adopt them," Sister said. "Maybe we can tell them about that, too."

Daddy yawned and said, "Yes, we will tell them all about our long ride. But right now, let's go to bed."

The next day the family went on a long ride together, and after three bus rides, four long airplane rides, and a tan van ride, they arrived on the other side of the ocean at a house called "home."

The long ride had ended, and the new life together had begun.

–The END–
(OF A LONG RIDE)

19

(TURN THE BOOK OVER TO READ
ABOUT THE FAMILY'S
LONG RIDE)

–The END–
(Of A Long Ride)

(Turn the Book Over to Read
About Li Li and Bei Bei's
Long Ride)

And that's just what they prayed, there in that big hotel on the other side of the world.

The next day, the family went on a long ride together, and after three bus rides, four long airplane rides, and a tan van ride, they arrived on the other side of the ocean at a house called "home."

The long ride had ended, and their new life together had begun.

After Bei Bei and Li Li were asleep, the daddy sat down on the bed. "I'm plumb tuckered out," he said.

"I'm tired too," said Mommy. "From all the paperwork! And the long ride across the ocean. And the money we spent. That would wear anybody out."

"Just think of what God did to bring us into His family," Daddy said. "We couldn't get into His family by ourselves, but He came to us. He traveled all the way from heaven to earth just for us. And at the end of His life on earth He walked all the way from Galilee to Jerusalem, to die on a cross to pay for our sins."

"God did so much work for us!" said Sister. "I used to think that because He worked so hard to adopt me, I didn't have to do anything. But there is one thing we have to do to be adopted by God. Right, Daddy?"

"Yes, that's right. We must trust God alone to save us, like Bei Bei and Li Li are trusting us right now. It's what the Bible calls 'faith.' It says, 'Saving is all his idea, and all his work. All we do is trust him enough to let him do it. It's God's gift from start to finish!' (Ephesians 2:8)."

"When we trust God, He adopts us into His family and makes us His very own dear children forever," said Mommy, with tears in her eyes.

"I sure hope God adopts Bei Bei and Li Li into His family," Sister said wistfully.

"Let's pray that He will," said Mommy.

A man in a fancy suit opened the big glass door.
They went inside and sat down to wait.

Soon a taxi stopped in front of the big hotel. And there,
outside that big hotel, they found what they had wanted
all along: two little girls with black hair, button noses,
and bright eyes as black as coal.

The daddy bounced Li Li on his knee and said, "Hupps,
hupps, hupps," while the mommy took Bei Bei on her lap
and softly sang,

"Be near me, Lord Jesus, I ask Thee to stay
  close by me forever, and love me, I pray.
Bless all the dear children in Thy tender care,
  and fit us for heaven to live with Thee there."

The mommy and the daddy and the sister smiled with
happy tears in their eyes. At last their family was complete!

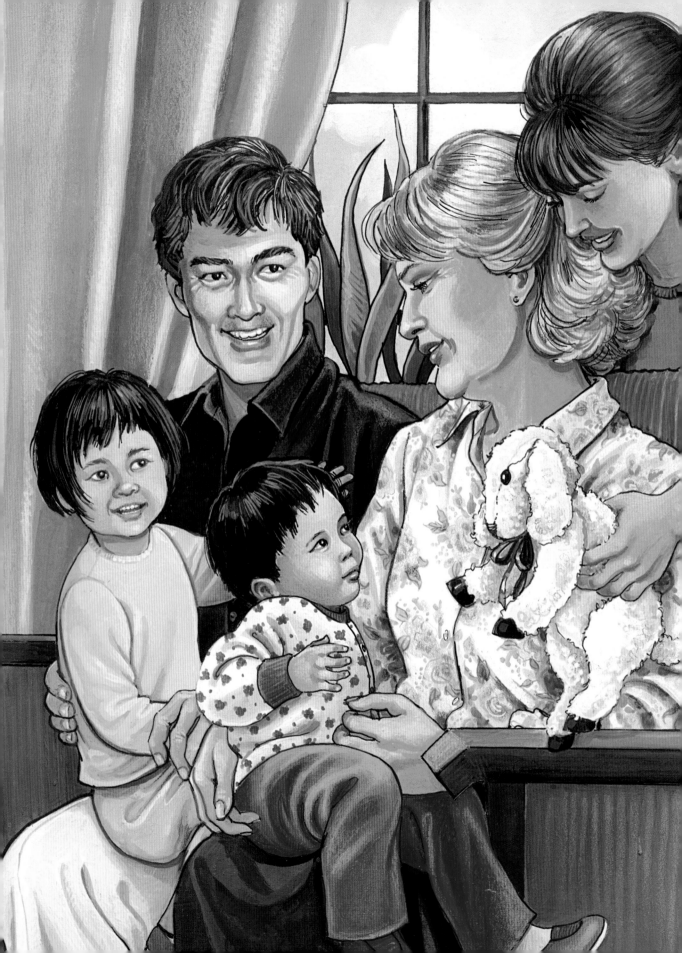

After they landed at the strange airport, they climbed onto a noisy bus. The bus driver tooted his horn so he wouldn't bump into the taxis or the people who were riding their bicycles in the street.

"I wonder if our girls are riding in one of those taxis," said Mommy.

Finally they arrived at a big hotel.

When they reached the other side of the world, the flight attendant gave them a special treat to eat.

"How can I eat noodles with sticks?" asked Daddy.

"Those are chopsticks, sir," the flight attendant said, and she showed him how to use them.

"What do you think Bei Bei and Li Li are doing right now?" Daddy asked.

"I think they're going to bed," said Sister.

Mommy said, "I hope someone will give them a hug."

At last the airplane landed in the biggest city they had ever seen. They met other families who didn't have babies, but who wanted them so much that they would go anywhere in the world to find them. Then all of the families flew far away together on another airplane.

The daddy looked out the window and wondered if his little girls were riding on the train that he saw far below. "Soon they won't be orphans anymore," he thought.

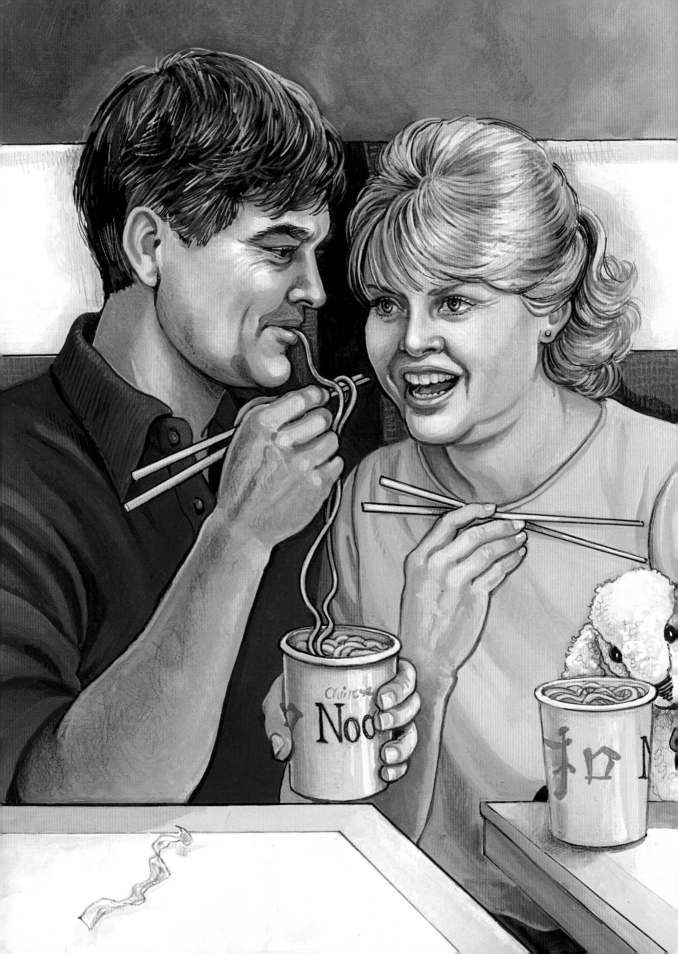

Early one morning, the daddy awakened the sleeping mommy and sister. "Come on, sleepy-heads," he said. "Let's go to the airport. It's time for the long ride to the other side of the world to adopt Bei Bei and Li Li."

They climbed into the tan van and took a long ride to the airport. The daddy counted all the suitcases over and over again. The mommy held on tightly to her paperwork.

They stepped aboard an airplane and flew far away. When they had flown as far as they could, they got on a different airplane that was bigger than a house. All day they flew on that airplane. When they looked out the window, all they could see were clouds and the big ocean under them.

"Are we there yet?" asked Sister.

"No," said Mommy. "Why don't you just watch the movie?"

"But I've seen it three times already," said Sister.

"Why don't we all try to sleep," said Daddy.

They tried to sleep, even though it was still daytime. It was the longest day and the longest ride they ever knew.

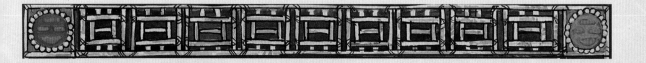

When the daddy came home at night, the mommy was still doing paperwork. "I almost have all the papers notarized," she said one night. "Next I must get the notarized papers authenticated."

"Those sure are big words," said Daddy. "I hope we can get a baby with all this work. Do you think we can get two babies?"

One day a social worker came to visit. She thought they were a good family for a baby. This made the mommy and daddy very happy.

At last Mommy finished the paperwork.

One day, the telephone rang. The social worker said that they could adopt two babies named Bei Bei and Li Li. This news made the family very excited. Those were the two little girls they wanted.

The daddy decided that the boys would stay home and watch the house. Then he would take a long ride with the mommy and the sister to adopt Bei Bei and Li Li. They stuffed their suitcases full of clothes, toys, and vitamins.

Then they sat down to rest.

Once upon a time, in a place not too far from here, there lived a mommy with golden hair and a daddy whose hair looked like salt and pepper.

They lived in a house with their four children, mostly boys. They were thankful for their family—for their big boys and their daughter. But something was missing!

They didn't have a baby.

The mommy didn't have a baby to sing to. The daddy didn't have a little girl to bounce on his knee, and the brothers and sister didn't have a little sister to take to the ice-cream store.

Every day the daddy went to work, but the mommy stayed very busy at home. She called it "paperwork." She wrote words and signed her name on papers. She sent money to people. She made telephone calls to people far away, and then she waited for them to call her back.

-The- Long Ride

A Family's Search

Don Regier

Illustrated by Karen Pritchett

Where Kids are number One